Published by Yali Books, New York

Text copyright © 2017 by Mamta Nainy
Illustrations copyright © 2017 by Siddhartha Tripathi

Connect with us online -
www.yalibooks.com
Instagram / Twitter / Facebook (@YaliBooks)
Pinterest (@yali_books)

ISBN: 978-0989061568

MILKY WAY

STORY
MAMTA NAINY

ILLUSTRATIONS
SIDDHARTHA TRIPATHI

yali books

Tashi loved the room in his house with the big window.

Every night after dinner, he would sit by the window and listen to the distant sounds of the gongs from the *Gonpa*...

...or gaze at the mountains covered in velvety darkness...

...or mimic the purring of a house cat that sat outside...

...or call out "Julley!" to
village folk returning from
Leh by the evening bus.

But what Tashi enjoyed doing the most was staring into the deep blue night sky.

When he looked up at the stars,
he felt as if they were talking to him.

Tashi was friends with all of the stars,
but the roly-poly moon was his favorite.

He once told his grandmother, "Momo-ley, the moon looks at me and gives me a special smile—eyes closed and no teeth showing."

"You and your stories, Tashi!" Momo-ley had said, pinching his cheeks.

One night, as the old wind-up clock chimed eight, Tashi went into the kitchen where his mother, Amma-ley, was laying out dinner.

He took his usual place on the floor next to Momo-ley, as Amma-ley served them bowls of steaming-hot *thukpa* topped with yak cheese.

Tashi quickly polished off his dinner and headed straight for the room with the window.

He was busy talking to the stars when the
big round moon glided in and sat upon
a branch high up on a juniper tree.

"Julley!" Tashi greeted the moon. "Why are you so late?"

"Well, Tashi, remember how the sun comes in to wake me up every night?" asked the moon.

19

"Today, he met some clouds on his way home and started to play with them. When he finally got back, it was quite late, you know," Tashi heard the moon say.

"Sometimes when I'm playing with Choden and Stanzin, I forget to do my homework and Amma-ley scolds me. Didn't the sun's Amma-ley scold him?" Tashi wanted to know.
But the moon just smiled his special smile—eyes closed and no teeth showing.

21

Every night,
Tashi would wait
for the moon.

And every night, his
friend would make
his way up to the
top of the juniper
tree and sit there
to chat with him.

Watching the moon huff and puff his way up to the topmost branch one night, Tashi thought that the moon was looking thinner than usual. Or, was he just imagining it?

A few nights later, the moon looked half his size! "Why have you become so thin?" a worried Tashi asked the moon.

The moon in reply just smiled his special smile—eyes closed and no teeth showing.

The next day, Tashi waited impatiently for nightfall. Amma-ley had made his favorite *momos* for dinner but he was too distracted to enjoy them.

Tashi rushed through his dinner
and went straight to the window.

He saw the stars winking and twinkling as usual, but the moon was nowhere to be seen—not even the thin pale slice in the sky from the night before.

He waited and he waited but the moon did not appear.

Tired, Tashi went to his Momo-ley.

At this hour, he usually heard the *gur-gur* sound of butter tea that Momo-ley made after dinner. But tonight, Momo-ley was holding a glass of hot milk, covering it gingerly with the edge of her *chuba*.

"Why aren't you having *gur-gur* tea, Momo-ley?" he asked.

"It's New Moon Night tonight, Tashi," said Momo-ley, patting his head gently.

"On this special night, we remember the great Buddha by fasting and praying. We can drink only a glass of milk at night. You know, milk gives us lots of energy and strength."

A thought crossed Tashi's mind—
"Maybe the moon is getting weak
because he doesn't drink milk!"

From the next evening on, he left a tall glass of yak milk on the window sill for the moon to have his fill.

Little by little, the moon got his roly-poly shape back.

And then one night, the moon appeared exactly as before—a perfect round!

"My full moon is back!
My round moon is back!"
cried Tashi as he hopped
and clapped in joy.

37

The next morning, as Tashi was still dreaming, the little house cat on the window purred happily. She burped a HUGE burp and winked a BIG wink!

And as for the moon—you know what he did, don't you? He just smiled his special smile—eyes closed and no teeth showing.

Glossary

Gonpa - A Buddhist monastery

Julley! - 'Hello!' in the Ladakhi language

Momo-ley - Grandmother

Amma-ley - Mother

Thukpa - Noodle-soup

Momos - Dumplings

Gur-gur tea - Butter tea made in Ladakh by churning tea, salt and yak butter. The churning makes a *gur-gur* sound

Chuba - A traditional garment worn by Ladakhi women

About Ladakh

Note for teachers and parents

Ladakh is a mountainous district in the northern state of Jammu and Kashmir, India. Nestled in the Himalayas and bordered by Tibet, it is one of the highest inhabited regions in the world. Over half of the Ladakhi people follow Tibetan Buddhism and the landscape is dotted with monasteries and colorful prayer flags. Its largest town is Leh.

Visit our website to download a lesson plan. Additional links and resources can be found on Pinterest (@yali_books).

CPSIA information can be obtained at www.ICGtesting.com
Printed in the USA
LVIW01n1906181117
556821LV00018B/198